To Craigie

with fond m[illegible]

joint inspection of over
80 holes in July 1983

My admiration has no bounds
for the owner of a genuine
family four-holer.

Bill.

THE
MASTER BUILDER

The
Master Builder

the sequel to

The Specialist

Charles Sale

Illustrated by Percy Vogt

PUTNAM
AN IMPRINT OF THE BODLEY HEAD

The Master Builder
is published in the United States of America
by The Specialist Publishing Company, Burlingame, CA.
under the title *I'll Tell You Why*

British Library Cataloguing
in Publication Data
Sale, Charles
[I'll tell you why].   The master builder.
1. Management
I. Title   II. The master builder
658   HD31

ISBN 0 370 30927 8

Printed in Great Britain for
Putnam and Company Ltd
9 Bow Street, London WC2E 7AL
at The Camelot Press Ltd, Southampton
First published in the United States in September 1930
First published in Great Britain 1982

PUBLISHER'S NOTE

Charles Sale was an actor who wrote himself a
stage monologue which became and still
remains one of the world's great bestselling
books, *The Specialist*. He also wrote and
performed this sequel, which proved just as
popular with his audiences and has sold by the
hundreds of thousands in his native United
States, but has somehow never seen the light
of day elsewhere until now.

You've got to study your customer and
act accordin'

THE MASTER BUILDER

Mr Chairman and Members of the Young Men's Business Breakfast Club:

Your chairman has asked me to talk on and point out such problems and pitfalls as confront the business man of today—and I'll tell you why. It's because he knows me as a specialist with thirty-two years' experience in my business. Everybody knows I'm the head of my profession. Only one feller ever disputed it, and I run him out of business, as I'll tell you about later. And the same things—*the very same things*—that made me a big success in my specializin', will be a big help to you, too, if you practice what I'm going to tell you.

I agreed to come and help you young men out, even if it is right in my busiest season, I'm just overrun with work—'course it's mostly repairin' on account of night before last bein'

Halloween—but I promised your chairman to come, so here I am.

Whatever profession you're in, gentlemen, if you are honest, sincere, trustworthy and give service, success will generally take care of itself; but there are other things very important too. For one, you've got to study your customer and act accordin'.

Take restless, fidgety, flighty customers—I'd sure lose their trade if I didn't know my business and use my head. It's my idea that the customer is always right; but with these undecided folks, you reach a point where you've got to be firm. Now with this kind of trade when it comes to location —they'll have me dig here, and then have me dig there, and then have me dig some other place. Finally, when things have gone jest so fur, I'll throw down my spade and say: 'Now I want to please you, and I'm here to build 'er. But we are wastin' valuable time pickin' spots; so you'd better make up your mind where you want her put; because all this diggin' is goin' to cost you money.' Well, that usually settles 'em, and I pin 'em down to a location.

From then on I've got the situation under control, and the job moves right along with no trouble— 'til it comes to the number of holes. If they start hemmin' an' hawin' around, tryin' to decide between a two and a three hole job, I always say to 'em: 'After the job's finished, I won't be here to make up your minds fer you; so we'd better make her a one holer—and I'll tell you why: When folks with undecided minds like yours, come out here in a big hurry, with anything more than one hole, you are liable to forget to figger in the extra time fer the decision. With a one holer the decision is made.'

Makin' a job fool-proof comes under the head of efficiency, and is something all business men should practice. So you see, gentlemen, the rule that the customer is always right don't always work out.

On the other hand, it don't pay to jump at conclusions; because sometimes the customer is *absolutely* right when you are dead set agin their ideas, figgerin' they are foolish and unpractical.

Take a customer I had in our town—a skittish, scary sort of woman, the kind that would dodge in the closet at the first clap of thunder. Dogged if she didn't insist on me puttin' up a lightnin' rod on that job I built fer her. This bein' out of my line, naturally I argued agin it, thinkin' it was jest a faddish notion, but finally I give in. About a week later, a bad electric storm come up, while she was out in there. I'll be slab-dabbed if the lightnin' didn't strike a tree in the yard, glance off onto that rod and go in the ground, savin' her life. When anything happens to a woman like that, it's jest like puttin' it in the papers—so the

news spread. Result was, her talkin'
created such a demand that now all
my customers that can afford it, want
their jobs lightnin' rodded. Of course
on new jobs, this comes under the head
of extra equipment—addin' a new
department to my business that pays a
v-e-r-y v-e-r-y pretty profit.

Now there was a case where the
customer was right. Puttin' lightnin'
rods on that job didn't weaken its
construction or spoil its looks. Fact is,
the shiny point and glass trimmin's
sort of set it off.

It always pays to give the customer
what he wants, providin' it don't kick
back on you, givin' your business a
black eye—and I'll tell you why.

You take novelty ideas, like fancy
shingle work, stucco, lattice-covered
jobs fer vines, weathervanes, fancy
hooks fer hangin' the lantern on at
night—all right fer the society climbers, who are always willin' to spend
money to make a show.

Now these expensive doo-dads don't affect the practical side of the structure at all, and make fer better satisfied customers. Fact is, there ain't anything that helped my reputation more, or gave me as much good advertisin', as that special job of ventilators I cut for Chet Jenkins. You see, he come from an old English family, was always pointin' back with pride, so I gave him his coat of arms—mighty difficult to cut, too—a allegater without any tail, instead of the regulation moon, star or crescent. Chet was so tickled with the job, he didn't notice how much extra it cost him—said it gave the place class and individuality. Things like that really help your business, but when a customer comes around with a novelty idea that ain't practical, turn it down.

I had a case with a feller that run an amusement park. His mind run to tricky contraptions fer playin' jokes on folks. Come to me with a workin' plan

All right fer society climbers

fer buildin' a breakaway job out on his
country place. Wanted her built on a
high knoll, in sight of his front porch.
She was to be of trick construction,
with the four sides hinged at the
bottom; held together with a secret
spring, and to all appearances look like
an ordinary, standard, regulation
three holer.

Here's the way she'd work: His idea
was to watch till he saw some guest
that was modest and high strung, go
out in there; wait till they got comfort-
ably located, and then call his other
guests to come out on the front porch
to admire the view.

Jest as they was all oh-ing and
ah-ing over the beautiful scenery, he'd
point at that knoll and say: 'Now
here's a view I always enjoy.' Then
he'd pull a secret wire, releasin' the
spring, and the sides and back of that
job would drop down like peelin' a
banana, and there they'd be— Well,
you can imagine the embarrassment.

Well, gentlemen, I turned his fool idea down flat. If I had been an inexperienced young man jest startin' in business, I might have done it and ruined my career. Danger bein', folks would likely have gotten the wrong idea—might think that all my jobs would fall apart like that, and where would I be? Certainly not standin' here today, the head of my profession, tellin' you young business men startin' out on a career how to make a success.

Now one of the most important items in buildin' up a business reputation, is the materials you work with. Take my work; when it comes to selectin' timber, I've built up a name fer bein' mighty particular. I never use anythin' but the very best clean white pine, with no knotholes—and I'll tell you why.

You take knotty timber—nine times out of ten, the knot will come in the door, and I've found out from my experience, that if it don't get pushed out, it will fall out; and the knot-hole generally comes too high to sit there and look out, and jest high enough for some snooper to come sneakin' around, peekin' in.

And it always pays to keep a good stock of supplies on hand fer special occasions, too. You take right after Halloween. If I didn't know how to figger in advance, I wouldn't be able to supply the demand for spare parts— such as new roofs, hinges, lost lids, catalogues, etc.

If the customer's contract calls fer a first class, dependable job, give it to him, and you can't fail. Even if you've figured a little too close, and stand to lose a little money—never use cheap material, and don't do any substitu- tin'. This goes to buildin' up your reputation, and once she's built up, you can always get your price.

Of course, if you're doin' a job fer charity, where there's no profit, you can skimp a little, and nobody'll think anything about it. Fact is, it's sort of expected.

Take the job I put up fer the Turtle Swamp Duck Huntin' Club. They got a mighty nice bunch of boys fer members—I belong to it myself; and they come to me, and asked if I couldn't throw together a serviceable, inexpensive one hole job, at jest the cost of the labor, usin' what material I could dig out of the ruins of the old club house that burned.

There wasn't much left but the tin roof, so I throwed them up a tin one seater—roof, sides, seat and all. She was shiny, galvanized tin, and showed up well at night agin the dark of the trees. Comfortable, too, till them frosty nights come along, and then the boys got to complainin' of that tin seat bein' jest a trifle cold. Suggestions passed back and forth, an' finally one of the boys spoke up and sez: 'How would it do to set the brim of a felt hat down in that hole?' They all looked at me, wonderin' what I'd think of it. Well, I figgered her out from every angle, and couldn't think of but one drawback, so I sez: 'Not a bad idea, if you can find an old velour with the crown cut out.'

Jest to show how that plan worked out, it got so that every mornin', right after breakfast, somebody would go out there, lock themselves in, and stay anywhere from forty-five minutes to an hour—leavin' the members to shift for themselves. Boys got mighty tired of this, and by checkin' up found out it wasn't any member of the club. They'd rattle the latch, pound the door, call, get no response, an' go away plumb aggravated.

This went on fer several days; finally one mornin', when they was all plannin' on goin' huntin' early, they got sick of the delay. Ed Smithers, who is always a master of any situation, sez: 'I'll show you how to get him out of there!' So he sends one of the boys down in the woods, about a hundred yards away, with a shotgun. Ed, sneakin' up, an' standin' about six feet away, with a hand full of gravel, yells: 'Don't point that gun this way!' (That bein' the signal to shoot.) 'BANG!' goes the gun in the air. Then Ed throws that handful of gravel agin the back of that tin job, and out pops a good-fer-nothin' feller by the name of Bart Wheeler, too scared to show his embarrassment.

Know what he'd been doin'? He'd been diggin' post-holes on the 'joinin' farm, an' secretly takin' advantage of the comforts of the Club. And that, gentlemen, will give you jest a slight idea of the caliber of the man. Yet, that same feller set hisself up as my competitor.

Now, fair competition never hurt anybody. You can always meet it half way, an' it stimulates business. On the other hand, unfair competition can cause you a lot of temporary trouble.

What was he?
Just a common post-hole digger

After one experience of gettin' stung by the feller that comes along, cuttin' under your price, usin' second grade material an' poor workmanship, folks soon find out it pays to get a man that has specialized and knows his business—from my profession on down.

Take this Bart Wheeler that jumped in on me. He couldn't be anything but unfair competition, because in the first place, what was he? Jest a common post-hole digger. I'll admit, that in soft ground he did dig a fair post-hole; but at that, he was mighty slow about it. Instead of bein' original, stickin' to post-hole diggin', perfectin' his work, an' becomin' a specialist in that line, he was flighty, an' jumped around from one job to another—out of work half the time. Once in awhile I'd take pity on him and let him do a little work fer me. And, gentlemen, there is where I made a mistake—although I only let him do the roughest kind of diggin'. Diggin' is the only part of my job I

don't like to do anyway, because when
the job is finished it don't show. Of
course, when it come to the squarin'
an' shapin' up, I couldn't trust him. I
always had to take the spade an' do it
myself. As fer him pickin' up a hammer or saw on one of my jobs—I
wouldn't have trusted him to build the
cob box.

Well sir, you could have knocked me
over with a feather when I heerd he'd
gone out an' bid agin me on the
Robinson job. He got it, too, by doin' a
lot of underhand price cuttin', an' he
didn't even know the first principle of
my work, which is the knack of pickin'
a location. When the boys told me he'd
picked a spot jest south of the house,
and right up agin the fence, I sez: 'It
won't work. I know the location well;
it's a right pretty spot, but it ain't
practical—and I'll tell you why: It's
too close to the road.' Take a woman
headin' out there; say there's some
boys drivin' by—especially in a

wagon with sideboards—they'll
watch her on the way out, and jest the
minute she gets her hand on the latch,
they'll yell: 'YIP Y-I-P!' an' dodge
down in the wagon. M-i-g-h-t-y
m-i-g-h-t-y embarrassin' fer the wimmin folks.

Gentlemen, sentiment in business
won't work. You see what it done to
me. Bart might have stuck to post-hole
diggin' and never set hisself up as my
competitor in a business he knowed
nothin' about, if I hadn't brought it on
myself, by takin' pity on him.

Take my advice, and never let your
tender heart get the best of your
judgment. It'll get you in a lot of
trouble like it did a friend of mine by
the name of Ed Clark.

It almost makes me cry when I think
what that boy went through. Big,
strappin' feller, great business man,
never sick, or lost a day's work in his
life. Had a good job as track-walker fer
the railroad, and was married to one of

the finest little wimmin that ever
swung a broom. Hard winter come
along. One of them cold mornin's—
must have been twenty degree below
zero—jest bitter—his wife got up to
build a fire. Ed was layin' there in bed,
watchin' her. Well sir, he's so sen-
timental that his feelin's jest got the
best of him. He couldn't bear to lay
there in that warm bed, and watch
that frail little woman up there,
shiverin' in the cold, buildin' that fire.
So he pulled the covers over his head,
an' froze his feet! A victim of a tender
heart, if there ever was one.

Of course a certain amount of sentiment is all right, especially with old
folks. That was one of Bart's failin's.
He'd take advantage of old folks. I
always done the work fer the Porters—
nice folks—raised a big fine family of
children. Well, their job was wrecked,
Bart rushes right over there, and bull-
dozed 'em into buildin' a three holer—
two big an' one baby, knowin' all the

A victim of a tender heart if
there ever was one

time their children are all gone away, and a one holer would have been plenty big enough, an' saved them money. Now, jest think what a low-down, ornery trick that was. There's them two feeble old people, both past eighty, left alone with the extra work, upkeep, an' expense of an eight family job.

To top it all off, Bart went around town, chest stickin' out, braggin' about it. Claimed it showed sales-manship. He bragged so much, that danged if he didn't go out and land a contract fer a eight holer out at the Happy Hour Dance Pavilion—a big deal I'd been figgerin' on fer months.

He promised to have her finished fer openin' night. Did he do it? No sir; he didn't even get the roof on. The next thing he done, was bungle up the doors. When they started ridin' him, he got nervous—jest when he ought to use his head—and not knowin' his business, he started takin' advice from everybody—the very worst thing you can do in any profession. He asked the entertainment committee what size they wanted the holes cut. By that time, they was plumb disgusted with him. So Filbert Twitch, who works down at the general store, sells hats and is always smart Aleckin' around, sez: 'Oh, cut 'em the regulation size, six and seven-eighths.' And danged if he didn't take him seriously, an' do it. Jest as I expected, the floor manager of the pavilion come rushin' in to see me fer expert opinion. I listened, polite-like, till he finished explainin' their predicament, then I sez: 'Well from your description, way I look at it, you've got yourself a good job fer kids, but as fer grown folks, if they can get in at all, they've got to be m-i-g-h-t-y m-i-g-h-t-y cautious.'

There was a case of salesmanship wasted—through lack of experience to back it up.

Course, a young feller startin' out

in business, can't have experience to begin with. He's got to pick it up as he goes along, but if he runs into somethin' that's too hard a nut fer him to crack, he can't afford to take advice from jest anybody, or start experimentin' on his own hook. If he goes to some older business man, and gets the benefit of his advice, it'll keep him from goin' off half cocked over new ideas.

Take the fad of comin' out with new models every year. In some lines it's all right an' stimulatin' to trade; but in my business, it ain't practical—and I'll tell you why. Jest when you think you've got a new model that's perfect, some weakness will crop out, like these new fangled slidin' doors—they always stick when you ain't expectin' them to, throwin' the whole plant out of commission. And by the time you get things fixed up, you've lost a lot of customers.

My system is to stick to the standard

type—addin' every year, such improvements as I've tried out and found foolproof. Some of my very first models are still givin' satisfactory service, with very low upkeep.

Experimentin' around is liable to prove costly—and it's the customer that pays fer it in the long run.

Take the Hubbards over in my town. Bart Wheeler's experimentin' cost them folks a cool $25,000—and it was a danged shame, even if they didn't ask me to bid on the work because somebody blackballed Sim Hubbard in the lodge. They was figgerin' on a job, to be put on a vacant lot in back of their place, that could be moved in case they sold the property. Well sir, Bart was stumped. Instead of goin' ahead with a regulation job, with temporary anchorin', he figgered around all one mornin' tryin' to solve their problem of movin' it easy. Along about noon, he went over to the lunch wagon to get a bite to eat, and there hc got the bright idea of puttin' her on wheels. And dogged if he didn't sell the Hubbards on it, too.

When he got her finished, the first feller to try her out was the Hubbard's crabby, rich, old Uncle Essley, who they'd been caterin' to fer years. He was out in there when a wind storm blowed up. The lot bein' on a slant, it didn't take much to start her rollin'. She moved faster and faster, headed straight down Main Street, doin' about thirty-five miles an hour, the door flappin' open and shut, the old man yellin', too scared to jump out.

'Suds' Morton, one of our most prominent citizens, who was crossin' the street with some washin' fer his wife to do, had to drop the clothes and jump fer his life. One of the wheels hit the basket, she slewed around, hopped the curb, takin' out down the sidewalk, and smacked right through the plate glass window, into the millinery store, full of wimmin. Out jumped the old

A tragedy on Main Street

man and not even stoppin' to apologize to the ladies fer the intrusion, he headed straight fer his lawyer, cut the Hubbards out of his will, and left town madder'n a hornet.

It's jest such work as this that makes it hard fer the builder that takes his work seriously and tries to protect his reputation as a specialist in his line. Some nit-wit will jump in tryin' to imitate him, cut loose with a lot of fool ideas, and do the business more harm than good.

Of course, any man can make mistakes, and they hadn't ought to be held agin him if he shows sense enough to profit by 'em. But not Bart. You would think, after one experience like that —feather brained as he was—he'd have knowed enough to watch his anchorin' mighty close. But no sir, gentlemen, give a competitor like that enough rope, and he'll always hang hisself.

He turned right around, only three

weeks later, and built a standard job
fer the bank, and danged if he didn't
fail to anchor it. Halloween night come
along, bank night-watchman hidin'
out in there, sawed off shotgun across
his knees, layin' fer the boys, expectin'
trouble. Boys didn't show up right
away, so he got tired waitin', and
through force of habit, falls asleep
asettin' there. Fatty Smithers, knowin'
the night watchman's failin' fer nap-
pin' on the job, located hisself in the
alley runnin' by the paint shop, back of
the bank. Upendin' a barrel of turpentine, and puttin' a box on it, he climbs
up to act as lookout fer the boys. As
soon as he heard the snorin', he give
the signal and the boys snuck over.
When the rockin' sensation woke the
watchman up, he knowed what was
happenin' but it was too late then, and
over she went—and there he was
trapped like a rabbit.

The watchman was so danged mad
that he completely lost his head, and

lookin' 'round fer an openin', he stuck
the gun through them holes, and
started firin' with both barrels—
BANGETY! BANG. A perfect bull's-
eye, jest as Fatty was bendin' over to
climb down off that box. Jumpin' two
feet in the air, Fatty kicked the box out
from under, and down he come, in a
settin' position, bustin' through the
head of that barrel. And there he was,
jack-knifed in, turpentine up to his
neck.

He started yellin', and the boys
rushed over to yank him out, but he
was wedged in there, tighter'n a drum,
the nails bendin' down. So they give
up tryin' to pull him out, and somebody yelled: 'Get an ax!' By that time
he was frothin' at the mouth, his eyes
bulgin' out like a hoot owl, and givin' a
big lurch, he busted that barrel like a
egg shell. Whoopin' like an Indian, he
passed the boys faster than a streak of
greased lightnin', hurdled the fence,
watchman and all, took out towards

And the story around town is, it took 'em
two days to catch him

the creek runnin' faster than a scared deer. And the story around town is, it took 'em two days to catch him.

The up-shot of it was, Fatty's paw sued the bank, and the bank turned around and sued Bart fer not anchorin' the job proper. And by the time they aired it all out in court, Bart couldn't have got a job buildin', if he had worked free and furnished the timber.

Well, gentlemen, that wiped out my competition and I've practically had a a monopoly ever since. But havin' things all your own way, has it's drawbacks too, if you ain't careful.

Got so, I couldn't go down the street without folks stoppin' to congratulate me on winnin' out, and maybe ask a little advice about their buildin' problems: 'What's the popular designs fer ventilators this season, Mr. Putt?' or, 'Do you still recommend the lean-to roof as most practical?'—or some

question they figgered could only be
answered by a specialist.

Well, I got to admit, I kinda let
success go to my head. I got kind of
haughty and full of pride, jest the very
thing a feller in business can't afford to
do. Course, pride in your work is all
right; but personal pride is danger-
ous—and I'll tell you why: You're
liable to ferget it's results folks is
interested in, and not you. Another
thing, pride will nearly always make a
feller over-estimate his ability. He'll
want to take in new territory, instead
of makin' the most of the territory he's
in. He'll reach out, and nine times out
of ten over-reach hisself.

Over at Durham, the county seat,
they had a problem that nobody over
there could handle, so they sent fer me.
Like a fool, I let it puff up my pride
and, big like, I sez: 'WHEN THEY
BUILD 'EM BIGGER AND BET-
TER, I'LL BUILD 'EM.' Course, I

had plenty of work at the time, but I dropped everything and went to look the situation over, and there's where I made a mistake.

Old man Durham, richest feller in town, place named after him, lived up over the bank. He's pretty lame, and it's hard fer him to walk down steps. Price was no object, but he wanted a job fer the bank, and one fer his own personal use—all under one roof.

Now I could have put him up a twin job, like the one I built back of the depot, but there was the problem of him walkin' up and down them steps. After a little ponderin' and thinkin' I sez: 'There's only one way to solve it. I can put you up a double decker, with railed-in walk runnin' out to the second story, right from your back door upstairs.' He was tickled to death with the idea, and sez: 'Just what I want. Go ahead and build her.' So I did.

Naturally bein' the only two story job in the state, it attracted a lot of attention, and people come fer miles to watch me put her up. Bein' the center of attraction, I got to puttin' in some fancy touches and extra flourishes, throwin' the hammer up and catchin' it like a side show juggler. This created a lot of favorable talk, and knowin' I had made my brag that she'd be finished Saturday at noon, the crowd collected early.

Well sir, to show you how carefully I'd figgered that job out, I was drivin' the last nail in the last shingle, when the twelve o'clock whistle blowed. I tossed my hammer in the air, givin' her a *double* twirl this time, caught it clean, and drove the nail in up to the head. The crowd cheered, and in the excitement, plumb forgettin' I was not on a regulation one story job, I slid off that roof to show off, meanin' to take a bow—like them actors do—fallin'

When they build 'em bigger and better,
I'll build 'em

straight down twenty feet—breakin' a
leg—layin' me up fer two months
right durin' my best season!

Pride goeth before a fall, gentlemen.
So in closin', I jest want to say that in
life, or in any profession or business, it
ain't how or where you start that
counts—it's where you finish.